# THE MANNING HOUSE SAGA

## ANN PINCHERA

*Peter*
*My Rock*

# ACKNOWLEDGEMENTS

One encounters many people as they go through life. Some will be just a flighting moment in time while others, though the time together may be brief, will result in a lasting impression that lasts a lifetime. For me there were three.

Many teachers influenced me as I journeyed through school but none as much as one particular professor at Fairleigh Dickinson University. At the time, the school had many professors famous and known worldwide. One such man taught us the history behind the language; the stuff you cannot find in history books. We were a small class of seven taking the course for the 2-year language requirement. While we waited for class to begin, he would tell stories of countries he visited and about his boyhood. The character in this book, the great-grandfather is my tribute to this man. Although much of the story is fictitious, the foundation is built on what he told us. It was only later, after the course was complete, did we learn the truth about the man that taught us Russian. Under his tutelage, we read excerpts some of the classic writers in the original language: Dostoyevsky and Tolstoy, and although it took me over a year original Russian version of Dr. Zhivago. To my professor, I owe many thanks who taught me not only my rudimentary Russian and Italian, but the meaning of humility, dignity, and the importance of a sound reputation.

The second person is now a good friend. We learned to laugh and cry over life's trials and tribulations. We laughed at the similarities between her Aunt Veronica and my own Aunt Irene. She has filled in some of the gaps I did not know about history of Soviet Russia and the beginnings of this country.  Recipes online are great, but she helped me fine tune some of the more traditional dishes she learned to enjoy in her youth. Although her influence is not obvious, she has helped shape some of the characters in my writing.

Last should be first.  I have known him all my life. As far back
as I can remember, I followed my cousin around. He, being older than I,
helped shape many of the habits I still have today. I remember him always
with a book in his hand. No, he not only carried it, but read it as well.
He told me, "if you carry a book, you will never be caught with nothing
to do." He was right and to this day, I still carry a book. As I got older, I
could enjoy the many quotes from Shakespeare with him. To this day, he
will still kindle memories of those days and quotes not forgotten.

To these people and to my dear sister, nicknamed Ethyl understood
only by us, and who I dragged through some awkward escapades of our
early days, I say thank you for inspiring me.

# BOOK I
# A HAUNTED HOUSE

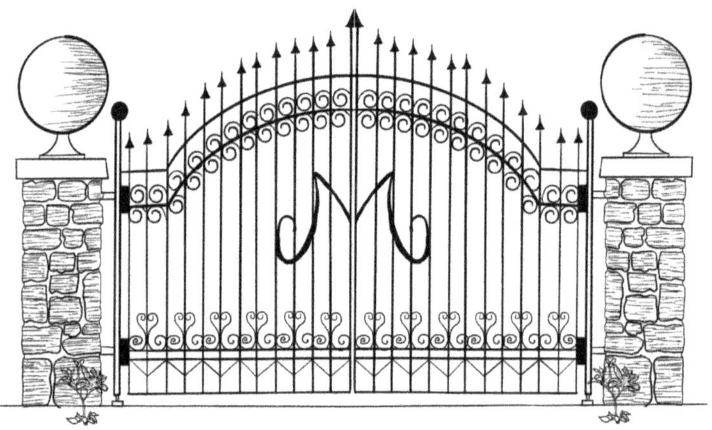

# CHAPTER 1
# THE NEXT ADVENTURE

Chief Davidson drove up the stone driveway to the front door of the Albright house and parked behind the black Honda. As he strode up the steps, his boyhood and still best friend Gus Albright opened the door.

"Guess who stopped by," said Gus Albright with a grin. "I was just getting ready to call you to see if you had a few minutes to stop."

"I was driving down Main Street and I thought I saw Ted's car go by. I figured he would be heading here first," said the Chief. "And, I figure he was here to see the boys."

"Yes, if that is OK with you gentlemen," said a voice from the kitchen.

Since the treasure map episode, the three men became good friends. Ted Turner's family were long residents of the town. Although Ted Turner was a few years older than the other two men, the friendship grew recently enabling Ted Turner to have a reason to visit town even more often.

"I thought I would see how the boys were getting on. Any new mysteries to solve?" said Mr. Turner with a grin as the Chief poured a cup of coffee from the pot on the stove.

"Nothing new other than homework," said Gus Albright. "Guess they have been too busy trying to get good grades."

"Yeah," said the Chief. "The library seems to be a favorite hang-out these days. I would have thought whatever they needed could be found on the Internet. But they seem intent on doing their research the old-fashioned way."

"Well, I'll be back a little later. I'm going to the cemetery while they are still at school," said Mr. Turner. "I'll leave my car here and walk since it is such a nice day, if that is OK with you. Don't want to break any laws," he said with a grin.

Mr. Turner jogged down the few steps and reached into the trunk of his car for a broom and a small bouquet of flowers. "Almost forgot these," he said as he started down the path to the cemetery.

Chief Davidson finished his coffee and handed the cup to Tom Albright. "I'll be getting along. I want to do some cruising around while the kids are on their way home from school. It pays to be seen sometimes. Call me if anything interesting comes up". Waving a good-by from his window, the Chief backed his car down the drive and sped away in the direction of the school.

# CHAPTER 2
# HAUNTED HOUSE

Corey and Bobby took their usual route from school passing by the old house on the hill.  In years past residents called it the Haunted House and the name stuck.  The house was a large mansion located on the highest peak in town.  From the front, the house appeared to be the traditional farmhouse layout however, the house even in its poor condition, indicated the owners were once very wealthy.  The fancy gingerbread woodwork around the porch was still intact although it needed a good coat of paint.  The house itself was brick and cement, which withstood the test of time and some of the very hard winters in Upstate New York.  Strong shutters with the exception of the attic protected all the windows.  The upper windows seemed small and difficult to see from the street and most of those windows seemed broken.  The lower floor windows were large and stretched from floor to ceiling.  A tall wrought iron fence surrounded the house allowing for plenty front of yard space.  From what could be seen from the road, an overgrown garden peaked from the sides and it looked as if additional buildings peered from the back of the house though it was difficult to see because of the distance.  A U-shaped driveway went from one side of the house to the other passing close to the front door.  On the one side was a portico and carport and what might be a long garage structure peeked blocking much of the view.  Unfortunately, the front yard was very overgrown making seeing what was actually on the property difficult.  Big signs hung on the columned fences at the entrances of the driveway saying, 'No Trespassing' and 'Private Property'.  In addition to the signs, it seemed there was the presence of an electronic surveillance systems. It was not known for sure if the system was real or still in-tact. No one ever took the chance to enter the property for fear of the nasty rumors implying the fence was highly electrified.

The house seemed to have passed into a vague recollection for most people. Most people in town hardly knew anything about the residents and only a few were able to recall some rumors of ghosts, the threat of sickness, or even death to anyone who ventured into the house.

The boys became fascinated with the haunted house when they talked to Mr. Turner at the conclusion of their Apple Tree caper. Although Mr. Turner said that was a story for another time, the boys were intent on finding out as much as they could before asking Mr. Turner again.

"I don't want him to think we are dumb," said Bobby.

"Dumb! Why would we be dumb asking him questions? Actually, I don't want him just telling us stories. I want to know the real truth."

"What's wrong with stories," retorted Bobby. "Sometimes they can be fun. Besides, what do you think you are going to find out? Do you think everything around here is a mystery? Remember, this is not New York City. This is small town USA. Nothing goes on here. Nothing!"

"So, why put a surveillance system on an abandoned house," Said Corey. "And when was that installed? Don't you think something is strange? Look, all I'm saying is we can do some research, like who owns the house, when was it built, who lived there.  That kind of stuff.  Public records have what we are looking for. Besides, we have nothing better to do."

"Yeah, nothing better than homework," said Bobby.  "I hate that teacher you had that put you on to Sherlock Holmes.  Now everything is a mystery."

"Nobody put me onto Sherlock Holmes.  I found it myself on TV. Then I found the books.  Besides, don't you want to be a cop like your father?  He does this kind of stuff all the time."

"I doubt it," grumbled Bobby as he followed Corey into the Hall of Records.  "I want to know how you are going to get away with this."

"Easy, it's for a school project," said Corey.

Once inside, the boys stopped at the information booth.  Not sure where they were going, the boys thought the best thing to do was ask someone for help.

"Look innocent," whispered Corey.

"Don't worry," Bobby replied.

"Excuse me, we are looking to find some information on a house here in town," Corey said trying to look as if he was unsure of his plan.

"What house, and what information are you looking for," said the lady before looking up at the boys. "Aren't you the Chief's kid," she asked Bobby.

"Ah, yeah, I am," stammered Bobby. "We are working on a school project and we aren't really sure what information we need to get started."

"Humph," grumped the lady. "Guess now I can expect a whole bunch of you kids in here. That's all I need."

"NO! I mean No ma'am. We each have a different project. We work in teams. My friend Corey and I are doing this project on an old house here in town," Bobby answered quickly.

"Yeah, and we thought instead of doing something on historic areas or battles, we would look into something a bit more modern and lo-cal," Corey quickly interjected. "We just want to find out things like who owned the house, and when it was built. Stuff like that. Anything that might be of interest to the class,"

"You must be the Albright kid. Right?" she said tilting her head to one side and running her pencil through her hair. "Heard you came back from the big city. Guess you have lots of places like that to investigate back there," she said with a sigh, "Guess you mean you are looking for information about the Haunted House on the hill."

Bobby and Corey looked at one another in disbelief. "How did you know all that? Corey asked.

"Look, kid, this is a small town and word gets around fast. Besides, it doesn't take a rocket scientist to figure out what you are looking for."

"You know my dad too?" asked Corey.

"Yup, they were always best buddies. I went to school with them. Well, not exactly with them, I was a few years behind them. Hope you kids aren't like them. They were always getting into some kind of trouble. Well anyway. Down the hall and to your right. That is where the deeds are kept. The lady in there will help you."

"Right, thanks," stammered Bobby as they started off down the hall. "Hope she doesn't see my dad and tell him I was here."

When they reached the door the lady indicated, Corey glanced back only to find the lady left her booth. Bobby turned the doorknob slowly. It was locked. On the glass was a small sign; "Out to Lunch". They sat down on a bench nearby and waited.

They didn't have to wait long when they heard the bolt pulled back. Bobby said to Corey, "Let's not hurry in. Give them a chance to get settled." They waited about five minutes before they tried the door again. This time, the door opened. They were greeted by a friendly smile. It was the lady they just talked to.

"IIello boys. Come on in. Now just what did you want to know?" she said with a grin as she sat behind the desk and the pencil tucked neatly in her hair.

The boys hardly knew what to say.  "Aw, gee, that's not nice," said Bobby.  "You played us."

"Yes, like a brass fiddle, as the saying goes.  So now tell me what it is you want to know about the Haunted House."

"Well, can we start with when it was built?" Asked Bobby.

"By the way, my name is Janice Henry.  You can call me Janice. Let me pull the records.  I'll be right back."

She disappeared for a few minutes then returned with a large ledger book dated the early 1900s.  She opened the book and quickly turned to a page and read, "The house at 1508 Hillside Rd was built in 1925 by one Leon Maternofsky.  The house has 14 rooms and is situated on forty-two acres of property and includes a barn, stable, servant quarters, and guest house.  The garage was added in 1928.  The pool was added around 1932 based on the assessor's records.  The house was never sold and remains in the Maternofsky family.  Taxes are paid annually from an independent source. It doesn't say by who or how they are paid.  All I can tell you is a bank check comes in regularly to cover the tax."

"You can tell all that from that page?" questioned Corey.

"No, some of it I know from being here so long.  You aren't the only ones curious about the house," said Janice.  "There have been a few people here looking to buy the property. But no records can be found as to who to contact.  The only thing anybody knows is that it remains in the possession of the family and managed by an attorney.  Exactly who and where they are is not known.  The only contact is a post office box for a law firm in Albany and they aren't giving any information."

Janice closed the book and peered quizzically at the boys. "So, now what?"

"Nothing.  We just were curious about it.  It looks haunted but nothing seems disturbed, as you would think a haunted house would look, said Bobby.

"Yeah," said Corey thoughtfully.  "I guess we reached a dead end."

The boys thanked Janice and left.  As the door closed, Janice reached for the phone.  Once outside the boys got on their bikes ready to head home.  Then Corey got a thought.  "Hey, Bobby, we really didn't reach a dead end.  We can check the newspapers and see if anything was printed about the house or the family."

"Oh, sure and where do you think you are going to start?  When the house was built? Or start with this year and work backward.  Do you have any idea how many newspapers that will be?"

"No, silly," said Corey.  "We can start around 1932, first go back a few years to 1928 or so then forward.  We know the pool was added then, so someone must have been living there.  Besides, for such a big house, these people must have been rich so they would be news especially society stuff.

"Good point," Bobby responded.  "I'm going to start looking on the Internet to see if anything pops up in the town history.  I don't imagine anything will be there because we would know it from school."

"Maybe so," Corey responded. "That's what makes it a good mystery."

# CHAPTER 3
# PLANNING TO MEET

They boys got to the Albright house just as Mr. Turner was coming from the cemetery.  As Mr. Turner got to his car to put his tools away, he saw the boys and waved them on.  "Been waiting for you," he said with a smile.

"We made a stop at the Town Hall," Corey said as he jumped off his bike to greet Mr. Turner.  "We thought we'd do a little research about the house before you got here."

"Oh?  Still wondering about that old house," Mr. Turner said thoughtfully.

Just then, Gus Albright came out of the house smiling at the boys.  "You have a visitor," he said.  "Are you going to come in?" he said directing the question more to Mr. Turner than to the boys.

Mr. Turner and the boys followed Mr. Albright into the house where a fresh pot of coffee sat on the stove, with milk for the boys and cookies were waiting.

"I can't stay long, but I will have the coffee.  Seems like someone beat me to the cemetery," he said to Gus Albright.  "I think your boys have been doing some work around the graves.  Looks like someone has been keeping the old place looking good and I saw the flowers on the door. Thank you," he said in the direction of the boys.

"Well, it was the least we could do," said Bobby, "especially after what you told us about who is buried there."

"I guess you really did listen to me about the stories and the old cemetery. You cleaned up the place really nice and the old graves look nice. Thank you," Mr. Turner said with a smile.

Gus interjected, "I had no idea that's what you guys were up to at the cemetery. I'm glad it was constructive instead of destructive. And, what's this about more?"

Mr. Turner said with a smile, "Your boys here asked me about the haunted house. I promised them an answer. But unfortunately, I can't do that now. It's too long a tale. How about I come back another day, say Saturday, and we have a long talk about the story behind the house."

"Gee," said Bobby, "I guess you know everything about this town."

"Not everything, but a great deal from my father. I can come back on Saturday if it is OK with you fathers. I'll meet you at the sweet shop – or whatever it's called these days." The sweet shop was the local hang out for kids who wanted to play the old 45 records and dance. The place retained its name but has modernized a bit with video games, action movies, and items more of interest to today's teen. One thing that remained the same were the booths and counter service for hamburgers, fries and ice cream treats to delight the palate.

Cory looked up pleading. "I guess so. It's OK with me. And, I think I can say the same for the Chief."

# CHAPTER 4
# RESEARCHING HISTORY

Cory and Bobby were not going to wait for the week to pass before doing some investigating on their own.  They spent an hour each day going through the newspapers in the library starting in January 1932.  By the end of the week, they completed almost five years and saw nothing of interest just some articles about social events such as birthdays and a yearly holiday gala.

"What kind of trouble are you two trying to stir up now?"  Asked Karla, a girl they knew from school.  She was carrying a load of books to-wards the shelf rack. Karla was in the same grade, but in a different class. Both boys worked on various science and math projects with her.

"What are *you* doing here," asked Cory a bit surprised to see her.

"I come in a few afternoons to help the librarian put the books away people take out and forget to return," she said.  "Is there anything I can help you with?"

"Nah, Bobby and I were just looking up some historical records about town. We thought we might want to use the information for a school project, answered Cory sheepishly hoping he didn't give away too much.

"There are no projects due," responded Karla in her best know-it-all tone.

"No sense waiting for the last minute, "said Bobby as he tried to hurry straightening up his papers to leave.

"I might know something about what you are looking for.  If you tell me what you need, I'm sure I might be able to guide you to the right spot."

"Thanks anyway," answered Bobby gathering up the few remaining papers and the boys ran off towards the exit.

As they left the library forgetting about running into one of their school mates, Bobby said, "When I get home, I'm going to look on the Internet to see if there is anything we can use."

"Sure, and how are you going to explain that to your parents?" questioned Cory.  "Don't you think your parents will be a little curious as to what you are doing?"

"Figured that out already, said Corey.  "If I am doing homework, I can sneak that in between searches.  I just want to see what comes up. Maybe something will give us a hint where to look."

"I have another idea," said Bobby.  "I'm going to ask my dad if he knows anything about the house.  I'm sure there must have been someone trying to break in or get onto the property.  He would know."

"Just don't get overzealous.  We don't want him to think we are, as the saying goes, getting into trouble. Remember what the lady at the deed's office said about them.  Besides, they already know we asked Mr. Turner."

The boys peddled off in the direction of home when Bobby suddenly turned and headed in the direction of his father's office.  Without saying a word, Corey also turned following Bobby.  "Hope he knows what he's doing," thought Corey.

Once in the office, Bobby said hello to the sergeant at the reception desk.  "Holding down the fort? Where's everybody?"  He leaned over waiting for an answer and toying with the paper clips in the tray.

"Hold on, bucko!  The last time you were here Grace had a fit and a half finding you put all the clips together.  She blamed me for the prank and since your father was standing right here, I took the heat."  Sergeant Williams was young and new to the force.  Recently separated from the Marines, the young man often sided with the younger generation giving them a break when he thought it was prudent.  Since he was a lifelong resident of the town, he might know something that would help the boys. The only problem was how not to tip their hand.

"Oh, I'm not going to do that again.  Not much fun if you can't see the end result.  We were just heading home from the library and thought we'd stop in to say hello to my dad.  Is he around?"

"No, the Chief went to check out a complaint about stolen pies then going to a meeting in the mayor's office.  I expect he'll be there most of the afternoon.  Want anything special?  And why the library on such a nice day."

"We are doing some research on town history for school."

"Oh, anything I can help with?"

"Maybe.  We are doing research on old families here in town.  Do you know who the oldest family here is?"

"Sure. That's an easy one," said the sergeant.  "That would have to be the Turners.  Next is a family that lived in the Haunted House.  I don't remember their name exactly, but from what I can recall, they were well off, employed most of the people in town in one way or another.  They had a son who was killed in the war I think, and a daughter.  Must have been something wrong with her because she was hardly ever seen.  Pretty thing, if memory serves me right.  Think her name was Alexa or Anna; something like that. Does that help?"

"Well, if my Dad isn't going to be back for a while, guess, we'll be going on home.  Better give up on the ice cream deal, Bobby," said Corey turning around to leave.

"Hey, before you go will you drop this off at City Hall for me.  Just leave it at reception.  It will save me a trip to the Clerk's office," Sgt. Williams said with a grin.

"Sure thing," Bobby replied and Cory grabbed the envelope as they ran outside.

It was not until they were on their bikes and out of the Sargent's sight did they stop to look at the envelope.  The writing looked familiar and was addressed to the City Clerk with a notation on bottom: tax payment.

"That's strange a tax payment would go to the police station," said Bobby.

"Take a better look," said Corey, "I mean at the return address. It looks as if it was dropped off and not mailed."

As the boys stared at the address, it read 1508 Hillside Road.

# CHAPTER 5
# ASKING QUESTIONS

After stopping at City Hall to drop off the envelope, the boys rode home in silence.  Cory and Bobby's friendship started many years ago indirectly resulting from the friendship the boys' fathers had as boys.  Corey, living in New York City, spent his summers with his grandparents.  He learned early to love the farm and the apple orchards.  When the workday was done, Corey and his grandfather would spend their time by the small lake formed by a nearby stream.  His grandfather put a wrought iron bench under a large oak tree then hung tire swing to one of the strong branches facing the water's edge for the boys to enjoy.  Although the boys talked as if they were too big for the swing, on hot summer days it came in handy to catapult them into the cool water.  Instead of going right home, the boys went to the small lake near the Albright house.  It was one of Corey's favorite spots.  Both Bobby and Corey enjoyed the memories and found it a good spot to reflect on the problems of the day.  The boys jumped off their bikes and sat in the grass near water's edge.

"I can hear those gears grinding in your head," said Bobby.  "What are you thinking?"

"Lots of stuff.  Mostly I have questions.  Don't you think it strange the tax payment shows up at the station today? We just went to the Records Office. I don't think the taxes are due just yet. It's as if somebody knew we were asking questions. But who?"

"Is that all?"

"It will do for a start," said Corey. "Do you have any thoughts?"

Bobby looked at the water pensively then lay back on the grass. "Yep. Do you think Mr. Turner is involved somehow? He was here and said he had things to do. Then the tax payment shows up. Was it him that dropped it off, and why at the Station House? It seems to me anybody wanting to pay a tax bill would go where they have to pay it and not at the Police Station. What's that about?"

"Not sure," said Corey. "Were you able to get time to ask your father what he knew about the house?"

"I started to, but the time wasn't right. He had other things on his mind. So, I figured I would save it for another time." A few minutes later Bobby added, "This seems to be a good time to ask since we took the tax bill. It wouldn't raise too much curiosity since the sergeant gave us the bill. Just curiosity I could say. Might give us another clue."

"Good idea," said Corey, "Just be careful not to get him too curious. He could shut us down in a minute especially if he tells my father too. Did you get a chance to find anything on the Internet?"

"Not yet.  I started with the house.  I didn't do a search on the name. Since the computer is near my father's chair, I do a search a little bit at a time."

"Know what you mean.  It's all a part of keeping us safe.  Did you hear about the girl in high school?  She was chatting with some kid and was ready to meet him.  Her mother found the thread and reported it.  Here it ended up a cop looking for stalkers.  She lost computer privileges for two months."

Corey laughed, "I got the scoop from my dad.  She was in eighth grade.  The cop was tracking the site and she was chatting with some guy before the cops took over.  Seems he was wanted in a few states for messing with kids.  My dad told me about it so I would be more careful.  I can't say I blame my dad, but sometimes I do just want to look up stuff without having to explain what I'm doing."

"Thanks for the real scoop.  She was dumb for even doing chats.  I hate to even chat with kids I knew from the City.  Never sure if it's really them.  E-mail works better and the phone better than that, not that I talk to them that much anymore."

Eventually the subject was dropped, and the boys started talking about the day's events at school.  Hearing footsteps, the boys turned to see who was coming.  It was Mr. Turner.

"Thought I saw you boys here.  Enjoying some quiet time before homework?" he said as he lowered himself onto the bench.

The boys smiled and swung around to face Mr. Turner.

"I understand you've been asking some questions about the Haunted House.  Did you get the information you were looking for," asked Mr. Turner?

"How did you know?  Who's got the big mouth around here," said Bobby with a grin.  "Did Mr. Albright tell you we were asking questions?"

"My father!" said Corey with mild surprise, "Why my father?  You have a father that's a cop.  I would think it would be your father who found out."

"Neither one," smiled Mr. Turner.  "Actually, I was just guessing you did some investigating on your own.  I just wanted to see if I was right." In actually, Mr. Turner got a call from his friend, Janice, who worked in the Clerk's office.  She told him the boys were there and asking questions.  They decided to see just how curious the boys were and Mr. Turner dropped off an envelope at the police station with instructions the boys were to get the envelope to bring to Janice.  For Mr. Turner, this would answer two questions:  how curious were the boys, and to what lengths would they go to get information on their own before he needed to intervene.

Bobby smiled, "I guess we fell right into your trap.  Actually, we did but we didn't find anything out that was of any interest.  We found out who the house belonged to and when it was built.  That's all."

Cory looked at his friend. What was he saying? They found out a little more than that. What was Bobby hiding from Mr. Turner.

Mr. Turner smiled. "I thought I would see if you boys wanted some ice cream before I headed back home. My errands didn't take as long as I expected so I thought I would see if you wanted a quick snack. Then I can tell you about the owners. I'm sure you are wondering about them".

"Sounds like a good idea. I'm always ready for ice cream," said Bobby. "I'll stop by the house to let my mother know where we are going. Do you want us to ride our bikes over?"

"I thought we'd walk. It's not far and I can tell you about the family."

Corey ran ahead of them and yelled into the kitchen then met them in the front by the road. As they walked, Mr. Turner started talking about the house. "You know my father was the banker and kept records about all bank business. The family was a prominent family and did a great deal of business with the bank.

"The family left Russia a few years before the first revolution," he began.

# BOOK II
# A HISTORY

# CHAPTER 1
# THE RUSSIAN BEGINNING

The year was 1901 in Imperial Russia.  Alexi stood in the bridle path watching his six prize stallions being walked back into the stables from the pasture after their exercise session.  He smiled to himself thinking about the wonderful job he did with raising them.  Soon they would be shipped off the buyer where such wonderful steeds were appreciated and well cared for.  Many of the horses he raised were sold to the officers in the Russian military, but he did raise better breed horses for the aristocracy of Asia and Europe.  Alexi looked up at the sky as the last stallion was led into the stable followed by the head groomer.  "Any instructions today?" asked the groomer expecting to hear any additions to the regular regime the horses got.

"No.  Just the usual," answered Alexi.

"Is something wrong?" asked the groomer.

"No.  I just feel a change is in the air," he said slowly indicating the weather.

Alexi was himself part of the aristocracy being a cousin to the Tzar.  He wasn't really fond of his cousin who was rather introverted making it appear he thought himself better than the others.  The other part of the problem was nobody, family or the people, really liked his wife.

Alexi left the capital with the excuse he needed to be with the horses he raised and without his supervision their training would not be complete or go as well as he demanded.  In many ways, he was a perfectionist taking pride in all that he did.  Being more in the country and not under the watchful eye of the Tzar, he heard many of his neighbors complain about the direction the country was taking.  The change he really feared was coming in the form of revolution.  That he did not want to see and started to think of ways he could distance himself even more from the government, his place in society, and the ruling family.

Slowly, Alexi walked down the path leading to the house with his head down and deep in thought.  He walked through the house into the great room and sat in front of the fire.  Rena, his wife, came in and stood by his side.  "What's wrong,"

"I fear times are changing.  I think we should make some preparations for the future.  I hear things, Rena, and they are not all good."

"I know your cousin can be a bit headstrong.  But the people have long accepted him that way," she commented trying to make him feel easy.

"It's not so much him as it is that woman," he said.  "I fear she will bring ruin down on him and all who are connected with the family.  Now I hear she is impressed with a monk.  Some fake from the wastelands."

"Don't talk like that about the religious," she warned. "It does not sit well with God. Please make a silent prayer and say you are sorry," she said.

"You do it for me. It's not that I do not believe. It's just from what I hear he is not a real religious man and more of an opportunist," Alexi said frowning. "I want nothing to do with him. Promise me, Rena, you will not get involved with this man," he said turning to his wife and taking her hands in his. "I hear many of the women at court are also going to him. He is no good. Stay away from him."

Rena smiled. "As you wish. But, now come in for lunch. Do not let the children see you like this. You know how impressionable they are." Alexi dropped his head and nodded. Slowly he got up from his chair and followed his wife into the dining room for lunch. The children, three boys and a girl, chatted happily about the day's activities and plans for the afternoon.

Rena and Alexi walked into the dining room where their four children were already seated. Tanya, the next to youngest jumped up to greet her parents exclaiming, "Papa, I am going to get my first riding lesson this afternoon. Peter and young Gregor are going to help me." Alexi smiled down at his daughter placing his large hand on her head and leading her to her seat at the table. Alexi said very little through lunch almost toying with his food. He was preoccupied with thoughts as to how best to protect his family in the days to come.

After the meal was over, Alexi walked slowly toward the stables where his prize stations were housed. He looked up at the sky which showed signs of an impending storm.  Not only the sky shows a storm, I sense a storm on the horizon, he mused.  In the meantime, a plan was beginning to take form in his mind.

# CHAPTER 2
# THE PLAN

As Alexi walked towards the stable where he was met by his stable master, Gregor. Alexi and Gregor were born and were together even though one was part of the aristocracy and the other not. Gregor's mother Olga was the family's housekeeper when she married. Olga and Alexi's mother both being the same age found they had much in common and often late in the afternoon, could be found sitting working on some sewing projects for the house or family. Both women gave birth to sons the same day and it was easy to see the boys playing together at an early age. As a result, the friendship between Alexi and Gregor ran deep, and each was devoted to the other. Gregor saw the concerned look and blocked Alexi's path. For all outward appearance, Gregor played his role as servant well knowing full well that was not really the case.

"I have something I need you to do," said Alexi. "We need to make some plans. Take your eldest boy and go to the Balkans and search out a farm that would be good for the horses. I also want you t to look into getting some other stock, like Clydesdales. They need to be good blood. You know the kind. We will be moving the stallions to the place you find saying we are loaning them out for breeding."

Without a word, Gregor smiled an acknowledgement. "What name shall I use."

"Yours," answered Alexi.  Make sure there are at least 2 houses, one for each of us.  I will be instructing my attorney to supply you with everything you need," said Alexi.

Gregor stood looking at his friend and master.  He knew something serious was bothering him.  "I will do as you ask," he responded.  Nothing more needed to be said.  Both men knew the plans were being made for all of them.

Many times, both men talked of the changing times.  Alexi felt some animosity towards them when the family visited the town.  It seemed to him there was resentment towards his station in life even though he tried hard to help those who were in his charge.  Since Gregor was not of noble birth, he heard many of the conversations and brought back news to Alexi that was not in print.

From distant villages, Gregor heard some villagers were being turned out of their houses and property they owned for many years, even generations.

"The seeds of revolution are being sewed," he once told Alexi. "As long as trouble stays far from us, we may be spared". Alexi never forgot what Gregor told him.  That along with the growing unrest toward the Czar, Alexi was preoccupied with formulating a plan to protect both families.  The only option seemed to be to leave.

Alexi met with his lawyer a few days later.  He instructed him to supply Gregor and his son with everything then needed to lease or rent a large farm in the Balkans. He explained he wanted to invest in some other breeds which might be more suitable for farm life and possibly a sturdier breed for the military. When questioned further, he said he thought he might want to investigate raising Clydesdales which he felt were also magnificent horses. He also explained he wanted to keep his new venture under wraps as he was not sure how well many of the aristocracy would welcome such a change thinking he was lowering his standards for fine horses. The lawyer agreed. "I will do whatever is necessary to accommodate Gregor and his son. Are you sure you don't want to buy the farm outright? And who will be staying there. I can hardly believe that you and Gregor would be living so far apart, knowing your close relationship."

"No, Gregor is going to be setting things up and will be returning to us. You are right. Gregor and I have no desire to be separated. We are closer than most brothers," Alexi responded knowing what he said was in confidence. "I will be in touch."

Later that day, Alexi found his wife sitting by a window doing some needlework. She looked up at him and asked, "What's wrong or are you in the process of making plans." Rena's smile faded somewhat as she looked up at her husband. "OK, so what am I to do."

"Plans," he responded, "And this is what I want you to do. "I want you to make a list of all your fine jewelry. Start with your small pieces of jewelry. I am thinking of replacing the precious stones with fake ones that will pass for the real thing. As the pieces are replaced, take the stones, disguise them and sew them into new clothes for you and the children. The clothes should be plain and suitable for travel. The larger pieces we will have duplicates made of much lesser quality. Some of the fake jewels we will leave here for anyone to see." Before she could raise a question, He added, "I have reason to believe someone is looking to steal some of your jewelry and I want them protected. Have Gregor's wife help you if you need help. Confide in no one but her. Olga will be working on currency we will need. I am sure with the talents you both have, it will be easy for you to hide the money and jewels we will need to get along." Alexi said quietly.

"I am sending Gregor and his son out to find a piece of property for horses. It will be most likely in the Balkans. He will be renting the property in his name. It is OK to say I am loaning him the money if word gets out. Once he finds what we are looking for, we will say we are taking a vacation and join him and his family in the new location."

"You expect trouble," she asked.

"I only know times are changing. I hear things even from our own people here. I just don't want to take any chances. From what I understand a group calling themselves Bolsheviks are inciting riots and mean to cause trouble in the government."

"If you are so concerned, why don't you try talking to your cousin. I am sure he will listen to you," she said.

"I've tried. He listens to no one but his wife and the monk who is influencing her. I think it best we put some distance between us," he said. "I just feel it's for the best.

"I will tell the staff we are thinking of planning a vacation and will be closing up the house here for a few months.  I will give them no specific timeframe or anything until they ask and closer to the time we prepare to leave.  That should stop any curious conversations by the staff.  Then they will busy themselves with trying to find out which ones will go with us and who will stay behind," she said with a smile.

"Maybe you can tell them we are planning to go to the summer house, after our trip." he said.  'That is always one option. They know we do that in the summer."

Rena nodded in agreement and went back to her needlework. In the meantime, Alexi looked out the large window facing the beautifully landscaped garden.  Rena could tell he was thinking.  She said nothing knowing when he was ready, he would share his thoughts.  Right now, was not the time to ask.

# CHAPTER 3
# THE NEW HOUSE

After a few months, Gregor sent word he found property he thought was adequate for their needs. Alexi made arrangements for the rental and the began the slow process of packing up the families. No one was surprised to hear that Gregor and his family would be going with Alexi. The first to make the move were the stallions. Gregor's two eldest sons oversaw making the arrangements for the horses. After prize stallions were moved, the second group of horses made the move. The only stock being left behind was used for food or horses that were considered too old to be able to make the move and would be moved to the summer house later with the staff. Rena made arrangements with part of the staff to make the transition to the summer house sending a small staff to prepare the house. The rest, with the exceptions a skeleton staff, were told they would be rehired when the family returned. Alexi was careful in making his selection as too who would go and who would stay. He overheard some of the staff talking about the revolutionary Red army beginning to pop up along the countryside. Those who were most boisterous he made other working arrangements until the family returned. Those more dedicated to the family were going to go to the summer house. Slowly the staff was trimmed while the families made ready for their vacation departure.

Gregor's family, although apparently making ready for the summer property, traveled instead to the farm Gregor found.  The sone were the first to leave with the horses while the women made ready to join the men.  Gregor's transition was thought to be with the horses since Alexi trusted no one with them.  And so, the plans for leaving were firmly set in place.

Finally, the day came when Alexi and the family were to leave.  At breakfast, Alexi with the family gathered announcing what he hoped would be a fantastic surprise saying that before they went to the summer estate, he was taking them on a small vacation, a cruise of sorts.  This, he thought, would buy them see time and not be missed by any of the staff or other aristocracy.  Little did the family and staff really know they were preparing to leave Mother Russia behind.

# CHAPTER 4
# PREPARING TO LEAVE

All of the ball gowns were carefully packed to be sent to the summer house.  The precious stones that originally adorned these dressed were painstakingly replaced by glass with the originals being carefully masked and sewed into the linings of the plain outfits that were created for their short vacation.  Many of these new dresses and outfits especially the ones for the children were made of plain fabric lacking the quality usually associated with the rich.  Although the outfits were plain, the embroidery gave the clothes a more dignified look becoming to an aristocratic family.  These clothes were folded and stuffed into suitcases and trunks that would be loaded onto the ship for the short sailing vacation.

Rena managed the packing herself making sure that all the right clothes ended up where they should.  Some of the more fancy and wintery looking gowns would be left behind.  Rena looked over some of her most favorite gowns being left with some sadness.  In some ways she would miss the pomp and circumstances associated with the royal family parties but not being summoned at a moment's notice into service by the Czarina.  The two, although distant cousins, having nothing in common, did not get along.  Rena got along well with the other court ladies and said very little in front of anyone of her true feelings.  It was one of the reasons she spent so much time at her home and away from Court.  Alexi too had little in common with his cousin though for all outward appearances they got along.  "The woman has changed him," he would say about the more shy and retiring ruler.  "Made him more of a bully."

It took more than a year to make their planned escape.  Finally, in a few days they would be leaving.  Alexi purchased tickets on a cruise ship sailing for the upper regions toward Norway before returning them for the trip to their summer house.  Unbeknown to anyone except Gregor and Rena, the trip would be cut short where they would leave the ship for the trip to the Balkans and their new home.  Only Gregor and Alexi knew the Balkans would serve as a temporary home before moving on into central Europe.  The house Gregor rented was for six months with options although he was already beginning his search for a new location in central Europe.

After a hardy breakfast and a last look around to make sure everything was in order, the family made their farewells to the remaining staff and climbed into the carriages taking them to the ship.  The younger children and the three eldest of Gregor's daughters who were going to help take charge of the children during their trip rode in the first carriage.  The rest of the children climbed into the second.  Alexi followed Rena into the last carriage.  He was the last to get in making sure everything was finally in order.  With a final look at the family home, he prepared to leave Mother Russia behind.  The Bolsheviks were gaining in strength and trouble moving closer to their home.  He knew this was the end and that he would never be able to return.

# BOOK III
# MEETING THE FAMILY

# CHAPTER 1
# MOVING THROUGH TIME

Mr. Turner looked at the boys. They were sitting across from him mesmerized by to what he was telling them. The ice cream in their dishes was all but melted.

"Boys," said Mr. Turner, "you hardly touched your ice cream."

"Wow! That as something. So, what you are saying is that the people that owned this house really came for Russia and settled here."

"When they left, did they come right here?" asked Bobby.

"No," said Mr. Turner, "They first went to the Balkans then moved around a bit. Alexi was afraid if they were found they would be forced to go back. He heard of the peasant uprisings and finally the revolution. He didn't want to get involved with any of the problems caused by the Czar. He was really afraid for his family and thought the best thing was to keep moving around and maybe they would get lost in the shuffle.

"For a very long time, they lived in Austria then, just before the outbreak of World War II, they moved again to France then Switzerland."

"When did they come here," asked Toby. "The only thing we

could find was around the 1930s."

"Alexi got very sick and was no longer able to do anything to help his family so he told Gregor to move everyone here to the United States where he felt they would be safe from any kind of retaliation from the Russian government.  They all came here in the mid 1920s just after the end of World War I, horses and all.  Shortly after they got to the US, Alexi died.  The oldest son, Petya took control of thing picking up here his father left off.  He was a lot like his father and with their newfound freedom, the two families almost lived as if they were one having been together for so many years.  Anna, the eldest daughter married one of Gregor's sons.  After both fathers died, Anna and Nikita moved back to France.  They found a vineyard and decided to make wine."  Petya married into a well-to-do family from Austria.  Both Petya and his wife liked this country enough to stay.  They continued to raise horses.  The youngest son, Alexi, also stayed in New York and went to school.  He studied European history and became a professor in one of the major NY City universities.  He also married and his wife liked the quiet life here in NY State.  She liked to cook and do very intricate needlework like Rena and Olga taught her taking up where they left off.  Some of er work was so good, it became fashionable to wear. Much of what she did was sold in expensive boutiques."

The boys just sat almost mesmerized by the story.  "So, the family is still here," said Toby.

"Yes," responded Mr. Turner. "But you understand that was many years ago and now the grandchildren and great grandchildren who are here run things."

"Do they still live in the house?" Asked Bobby.

"Wow!  Look at the time" exclaimed Mr. Turner signaling for the check, "I think that's enough for one day.  I better get you back home before you miss dinner, and I am in the doghouse with your parents." It was obvious he wasn't going to tell them any more about the family today.

"But we have so many questions," signed Bobby.

"I am sure you do, but I think we need to watch the time."  The boys packed up and got ready to leave while Mr. Turner paid the check.

"I have an idea," said Bobby signaling to Corey he had an idea. "Let's go along with things right now."

Mr. Turner dropped the boys off at the Alright home, said goodbye to the parents and prepared to leave.  "I'll see you next week.  We can continue the story then.  I am sure you have enough to think about for now."

# CHAPTER 2
# A SURPRISED VISITOR

A few days later the boys were in their favorite place at the back tables of the library. They hadn't seen Karla for some time. Seems every time they were at the library, she was off doing something else. Corey saw her first as she walked towards them with a magazine in her hand. She walked up to the table and very softly said, "I thought you might like to see this magazine." She dropped in on the table between the boys and turned to leave.

"Hey," said Bobby, "Where have you been? We haven't seen you even at school. Is everything alright?"

"Yes," Karla answered. "I've had some stuff to do at home. It's been a busy time for us lately and it seems my family needed everyone to pitch in."

"Anything we can do to help? We are willing helpers, you know," said Corey.

"Thanks, but no. We got it. In the meantime, thought you would find this magazine of interest." Karla smiled at the boys, put the magazine on the table and quickly walked away before they could ask any questions.
"What's that about," said Bobby. "She's never talked to us before."

Corey nodded and picked up the magazine.  It was an old publication from the mid 1940 and headlined up and coming mansions.  "Why would this be of interest to us" mused Corey.  "These pictures are mansions in California.  That's a long way from here."  Bobby grabbed for the magazine and thumbed through the pages.  Not finding anything of interest, he tossed the magazine on top of his school books.

"Why would she give us such a magazine," Corey whispered then went back to his reading.  Bobby just shook his head.

"She never talks to us," Corey continued shaking his head.

"Who knows.  She's a girl and you know they have their own reasons for doing things," answered Bobby.  "And look at the time!  We better get going or we will have to answer some questions when we get home."  The boys grabbed their books and stuffed them into their backpacks.  Corey gave a quick glance back to the table to make sure they didn't forget anything.  The table was empty.

"I always forget something when I'm in a hurry," said Corey.  I just wanted to make sure we left nothing behind."

"You would leave your head behind somedays, especially when you have other things on your mind."

The boys ran out of the library.  Karla watched as they disappeared down the steps and smiled to herself.  "Boys," she thought.  "Always in a hurry to go no place.

Peddling fast, the boys raced down the main street heading for home when Bobby came to a sudden stop.  They found themselves in front of the Haunted House.  Much to their surprise the iron gate started to slowly open to admit a car beginning to turn into the driveway.  The car looked familiar.  It was Mr. Turner.

# CHAPTER 3
# MORE QUESTIONS

The boys rode away as fast as they could only stopping when they put enough distance between themselves and the house.

"Boy, that was close," said Bobby.

"Did you see who that was?  It was Mr. Turner, and he was going into that house.  What was he doing there?  How does he know to get in?" cried Corey breathlessly.

"I don't know.  He knows more than he's telling us," said Bobby looking down at the hem of his jeans.  "Dang, put another hole in the leg of my pants.  Mom's gonna kill me," he said with a sigh.

Cory pretended to look interested.  "Look, I think it's time we got Mr. Turner to tell us all he knows.  Why would he be going into that haunted house."

"Unless it isn't haunted and just looks that way."

"Why would anybody want their house to look as if it were haunted," questioned Cory.  "Let's go back and see if we can see anything going on.  Maybe we can spot Mr. Turner and see what he's up to."

"Makes no sense," mumbled Bobby shaking his head. "Why would anybody want their house to look haunted."

They peddled back to the gate and tried to look in to see if they could see anything more than they normally could.

"By any chance, did you bring your field glasses," said Corey.

"Even if I did, do you think it wise to stand on the corner like this and try to look in.  I think we should find another place to see what we can see."

"Where do you want to go?  We might try around the corner.  Let's go around the house and really look to see what's there," said Corey.

"Can you think of any place that might be higher so we can look down?  It might give us a clue as to why Mr. Turner went in there and where he might be," Bobby said looking around.

"Higher?" are you kidding?  This is on the highest point in town, remember?"

The boys decided to ride around and see if they could see anything from the gate first, then checked around for a better place to look. After riding slowly by the gate so not to raise any suspicion, the boys rode to the sweet shop to talk things over.

They ordered a soda and sat at one of the tables near the corner widow.

"Sit here, and we can see if anybody is coming while we talk and try to figure this out," said Corey.

"You mean like Mr. Turner.  I can hardly believe he drove in the driveway.  I wonder if he did see us and pretended not to notice," answered Bobby as he stirred the straw around.  "We need to find a way to get in a position where we can see inside.  Something is going on there and nobody seems to want to talk about it."

"You lived here longer than me, do you have any idea where we can go to climb up and see what we can see.  Is there a hill or something, maybe a clump of trees that can help us see in?" asked Corey.  "Hey maybe we can use those field glasses to see what's going on inside."

"The field glasses are home and by the time I get them, Mr. Turner will be gone.  Let's ride around and see if there is something in the back of the house we can use to get in," said Bobby.  "Follow me."

The boys got back on their bikes and rode to the old house then peddled around as if they were on their way someplace else.  They quickly turned the corner only to find a stone wall on the other side.  Why didn't they notice this before?  They followed the wall to the end where it was met by high wire fencing around a field.  The boys left the bikes partially hidden in the grass by the stone wall and started to look around the fence for a place they could get inside.

The boys eventually did find a loose connection in the fence. They held it open so they could get on the other side and into the open field. They walked, rather crept, and kept looking around to make sure they were alone. Once out of sight of the road, the wall and fence ended and a wooden fence took its place. Carefully they looked at one another as if they found a treasure. Then they hoped the fence. In front of them stood the house and it seemed anything but abandoned. Suddenly a deep voice spoke from behind them, "Hello boys. Looking for someone?"

# CHAPTER 4
# SNAGGED

Bobby was the first one to turn around while Corey froze in his tracks. "Sorry, Mister, we meant no harm."

"I'm sure you didn't. But you know this is private property. Signs are everywhere saying 'Private Property. No Trespassing'. They are every few yards. I am sure you saw the signs especially with you being the Chief's son," said the man. He was dressed in a security company uniform. The man was big for private security thought Bobby. He wondered why a private security company would be patrolling the grounds, especially in what appeared to be an open field. The guard motioned for the boys to lead the way back to the fence where he parked his Jeep. On the back of the Jeep were their bikes. Cory could see the fear in Bobby's face knowing how much trouble he was going to be in with his father.

"Where are you taking us," stammered Corey who was almost as frightened as Bobby. "Are you going to take s to the police station?"

The security guard didn't answer, but held the back door open for the boys to climb in. Bobby whispered, "Boy are we in trouble now."

The big man walked around to get into the Jeep and drove off in a direction opposite from the road. He drove fast and the boys jostled around in the back. Suddenly he turned onto a dirt road with the field to the right and a track to the left.  The race track was well manicured and two horses could be seen on the end with a few men, one of which looked familiar.

The Jeep drove into a yard where two men were standing.  One was Mr. Turner.  The guard got out and opened the door for the boys.  Both men turned to watch them as they walked towards them. Mr. Turner didn't look angry and neither did the other man.  "Hello," said Mr. Turner.  "Boys, I'd like you to meet Mr. Manning.  He now owns this house you are so interested in.  This is Bobby, the Chief's son, and this one is Corey.  His family owns the apple orchard on the other side of the creek."

Both Bobby and Corey stammered a greeting.  Finally, Corey said, "We are sorry, Mr. Manning.  We meant no harm.  It's just that we heard so much about the house and we were curious.  We thought the house was abandoned and we just wanted to see what it was like."

Just then, a side door opened, and a nurse walked out wheeling a stately old man into the courtyard where the group stood.  The man sat tall and erect.  His thick white hair framed a jovial face with shocking blue eyes.  On his lap was a book whose title was written in another language lay open.

"I think you might want to call the young ones out here if you please," sad the elder Mr. Manning to the nurse.  "I think proper introductions are in order."

"Yes," she replied and went off into the house.

In the meantime," said Mr. Turner, "May I do the introductions?"

"By all means," said the younger Mr. Manning with a grin and slight bow.  The two men smirked at one another.  Mr. Turner started, "Corey, Bobby, I already introduced you to Mr. Gregory Manning, the current owner of this estate.   This gentleman is Alexi Manning.  His father built this house for his family after they came to this country and decided to settle here.  I do believe that is where I left off in the story.  Mr. Alexi was born in Europe and was the first to renounce his title when he applied for citizenship here.  You see, royal titles are handed down through the generations and although there is no longer any royalty in Russia, he made sure there was no reason for anyone in the government to follow him to this country."

The elder Mr. Manning continued, "You see, at the time my family left Russia, there were still many ties to the royal family.  The royal family fell out of favor with the people and many of what was known as the aristocracy tried to escape.  Everything we had to leave behind was taken by the state and distributed to the people. My grandfather fearing what revolution might mean to any members of the royal family made sure that anyone following our departure would give up eventually.  You see, the Bolsheviks known as the people's government wanted to make sure there were no family members that would try to reclaim the title.  Fortunately for many, civil war broke out and attention was turned away from our leaving.  After moving through several countries and with the outbreak of another war known as the World War, we came here.  The valuables and jewels were exchanged for currency to support our families.  We brought nothing with us other than clothes and the stallion descendants.  Here we started to raise our own horses.  Thoroughbreds.  Ah, here come the rest of my beloved family."

The door swung open and out came the nurse with a tray of drinks and fresh cookies.  She was followed by a young man both Corey and Bobby recognized from school. "I believe you might know my great grandson, Alex.  He heads the football team and will be going on to college next year." Behind him was a girl both boys new.  Karla.

"Karla," exclaimed Bobby. "Corey, shut your mouth, you aren't catching flies.  We had no idea you lived here."

"Nobody really knows where I live.  The principal at school knows, but as far as any of the kids or teachers at school, they think I live in one of the houses you see by the fields.  Nobody wants to think this house is really inhabited, so we let the myth go this house is haunted."

"Why haunted," asked Corey.

"The horses are valuable and because of the security cameras and stuff, people thought the house was haunted.  So, we let the idea go.  Besides, Grandfather here likes his privacy.  Doesn't need dozens of people asking questions."

Across the courtyard were the stables.  A beautiful chestnut mare poked her head out followed by one of the newest additions to the farm.  The little foal came running on unsteady legs and found its place close to its mother.  A young man called Ivan son of the youngest of the Gregor family came out. Behind him came the cutest Shetland pony. The pony came running to the group, nuzzled against the old man then went to Karla for a treat.

Karla said shyly, "My family breeds thoroughbreds, but my passion is the little ponies. We got the first one as a companion for Grandfather. I knew this is what I wanted to do, so I started researching how to raise and care for them. Now I have three ponies. Two of them are used for therapy and visit local hospitals for children. Ivan is the one who takes them since I am in school."

Corey turned to Mr. Turner and asked, "How did you get mixed up with this family?"

"I'm not are I like your choice of words," quipped old Alexi with a smile.

"My father got to know the Mannings from the bank. I went to school with Mr. Manning here in the early years of our education before he went off to private school. Our friendship goes back years and often I did the physical leg work for the family so they could stay quiet. After a time, well, it was just routine for me. Takes some pressure off the family and I am glad to do it. Besides me, Janice from the tax office also knows. She is Mr. Manning's sister's best friend."

The security guard went over to Mr. Manning and whispered something then left.

"Your bikes have been brought to the police station with a note that you are with me and I will be taking you home after.  I will talk to both your parents and explain how I took you for ice cream and had the bikes sent there so you wouldn't have to worry about them," said Mr. Turner.

"Are you going to tell our dads that we sneaked onto the property? Questioned Corey almost afraid to think of what the consequences would be.

"No," said the elder Manning.  "I see no reason to say how you got here.  I think for now it's safe to say you came with either Karla or Mr. Turner."

Alex turned to the boys and asked, "Would you like to see one of our beauties up close?  When you came in, you saw her on the track with the trainer and myself."

"I thought you looked familiar," said Bobby.  "Your back was to so we couldn't see you too well."

"I saw you coming and sent security to pick you up.  Mr. Turner told us of your interest, so it wasn't too much of a surprise to see you.  I just wasn't ready for you to see me.  Now I have to ask you for your word you will not speak of what you saw here.  We aren't ready for everyone to know who and what we do here."

Bobby asked, "How do you manage the farm?"

"Easy," said Alex. "The houses along the side street are owned by us. We allow our workers with families to live there as long as they work on the farm and care for the horses. Karla and I use the address of one of the more trusted families for school. This way there are no questions and any mail sent there is brought to the house. You see, many of these people have been with us for many years and they are loyal to the family."

Mr. Turner came walking towards the boys. "I think it's time we got going. Now that you know who the family is, I am sure you can see them at school and maybe become friends. It seems Grandfather has taken a liking to you boys and wants you to come back. "

"My grandfather is full of stories. He probably can tell you all you want to know about the house and the family. Our story is a rich one, if you like history, that is," said Alex. "I can tell you, but it is so much nicer coming from him. Besides, the accent adds so much richness to the stories."

Bobby looked at Corey and said, "We would love to hear the stories with you and your grandfather. There is so much we would like to know about the house."

"And the horses. Don't forget them," added Corey. "I think raising horses is so fascinating."

"You only say that because you think horses like apples, and you have lots of apples," chided Bobby. That made everyone laugh.

"What's so funny," asked Karla as she came back from the barn. "Are you laughing at my little ponies?"

"Absolutely not," both boys shouted together.

Alex added, "The boys were just saying how they would like to learn more about the horses. Real horses and not those baby things you have."

"My ponies are just as important. Just ask grandfather. He likes them," Karla responded to her brother. "My ponies are friends and companions to many who need a companion pet. Some of the ponies have learned simple tasks, like getting a blanket or going for help. Grandfather seems to be more comfortable with his little companion. He does go for short walks with him so he doesn't need to be watched 100%. I like horses, especially the little ponies. Besides, they are easier to manage."

"Maybe we can come sometime and help you with them. How many do you have?" Questioned Corey.

"Right now, there are five and one on the way," responded Karla. "I would enjoy your help."

As Karla was preparing to lead her pony to the stable, Mr. Turner and her father came walking towards them. Mr. Manning had some papers in his hand and what looked like a braided rope used to lead horses. "I thought maybe you would want to see one of our ponies up close. Remember now, these are young horses and bread for racing. You might find them a bit more on the wild side and they may not be as gentle as you think."

Mr. Manning led the group to the track where a young male was standing with the trainer. A jockey was already in the saddle. Mr. Manning said, "Each day and about the same time, we take the horse out for a run. They are not always run at top speed, but we try to get an idea of what the hose will do if raced. The runs are timed and averaged. As the times decrease, we then try to race the horse."

"Are all of these horses yours," asked Corey.

"Yes, but we do sell them and often the horse is sold before it's born. It depends on the parent or parents of the horse. Our horses are champion stock, so they are worth more. That's why I have to ask you for your word not to say anything. We do have security, but not to the extent some of the other farms have. We like to keep it that way," said Mr. Manning.

Looking down at his feet, Corey shook his head and said, "You must thing a great deal of Mr. Turner here. He never even hinted he knew you. All he told us was some of the history behind the house and the family."

"Bobby, don't you have any questions for Mr. Manning?" Asked Mr. Turner.

"Yes, just one. Are you really royalty?"

Mr. Manning smiled. "We can trace our family back to the royal family in Russia. Yes. But we are American citizens so we have no titles here. Only Grandfather keeps in touch with some of the aristocracy families who escaped Russia and during World War II. They meet every so often in the City. And, they have formed a sort of club. None of the families look to reclaim their heritage, just want to keep the old traditions alive here in the younger generations."

Just then Karla came up behind them. "Once in a while when Grandfather feels up to it, we take a ride with him. I love to hear the stories the people tell. Maybe one day, you can come with us, if Dad here and Grandfather agree."

Mr. Turner smiled at the boys. "Looks like you made a new friend. Now, remember, you must keep your word or you will not be able to ever come back."

The boys agreed and everyone turned to watch the young horse run around the track. Finally, Mr. Turner said, "Well, it's getting late and I better get you boys back to your fathers before there is a great deal to explain.

The boys ran over to Grandfather Manning to say goodbye. "Come again, he said with a smile. Karla needs friends her own age around. Then maybe you can help her with her pet ponies."

Happily, the boys turned to Mr. Turner. "OK, so now how are we getting out of here," Corey asked.

"I'll take you in my car.  Your bikes were brought to the chief's office with a note from me you were with me," said Mr. Turner.

After all the goodbyes were said, the boys climbed in Mr. Turner's car.  Instead of heading down the long driveway they saw him enter, Mr. Turner took some side roads and came out at the other end of town.  During the drive, they chatted happily about the events and the Manning family.  Mr. Turner again said how important it was to keep the family's confidence.  He told the boys they could visit Karla at the farm house next to the family property near where they snuck in.

"How did you get to know Mr. Manning?" asked Corey.

"We went to school together.  I was one of the few people who knew who he really was.  I found out by accident when I was doing a homework assignment on European history.  While in the library, I ran into Grandfather who was only too willing to share information.  Before he could finish one of his stories, Gregory came up to get his grandfather.  From that point on we became good friends.  There was only one other person who knew.  She is a cousin and is the only person other than the family that knows I know about them.  And, don't ask me who it is.  I will not tell you.

"I think I know," said Corey.

"Really, who?" Asked Bobby.

"Now what did I just say!" scolded Mr. Turner with a grin.

Mr. Turner pulled up in front of the police station just as the Chief was coming to the door.  He walked down the few steps to greet them on the sidewalk.  Holding the door open for Mr. Turner, he said, "I see, Ted, you found your young followers."

"Yes, and we had a talk all about the haunted house.  Now they know about it and gave their word not to disclose the secrets within," Mr. Turner said with a wink.

"Not even to their fathers who are just as interested?" hinted the Chief.

"Well," said Mr. Turner slowly as he rubbed his chin. "What do you think boys, you think your fathers can keep their secret?"

"Mr. Turner," said Corey slowly.  "I know we promised not to tell anyone, but I never gave my parents a thought.  I never kept anything from them before, so, if you think they can keep the secret, I would appreciate you letting me tell at least my dad."

"What about you, Bobby?"

"My dad's the Chief of Police.  I doubt he would do anything to put the family in jeopardy.  I think we can trust him too."

"OK, but only them and I will have to tell the Mannings what you said.  I am sure they will understand," said Mr. Turner.

"Mannings, THE Mannings," stammered the Chief.  Just as he was about to continue his sentence, Sergeant Williams pulled up.  "Chief, I just came from Mrs. Pollack's house.  This is the third time I was there with the same complaint.  She baked a pie and put it on the windowsill to cool …"

"And the pie was gone," interrupted the Chief.  "I told her time and time again not to do that.  Her pies are too good and hard to resist to any passerby.  Probably one of the high school kids or some passerby that we will never be able to catch."

Just then a long limousine passed by.  The limo was long and black with darkened windows, so it was impossible to tell who was inside.  The car moved slowly by as if the driver knew where he was going.

"Who's that?" questioned Bobby.

"Haven't the faintest idea," said the Chef looking at the sergeant who just shrugged his shoulders.

Both boys turned to Mr. Turner.  "You know everybody in this town, who was that!" asked Corey

"I have no idea.  No idea," stammered Mr. Turner looking at the Chief.

"Looks like we have another mystery on our hands," Corey said to Bobby.  "But this time we are on our own."